Little Red Riding Hood

To my analysands who have met the wolf — J. E-S.
To my mother Maria, who is both gentle and strong — N. C.

Barefoot Books
124 Walcot Street
Bath BA1 5BG

First published in Great Britain in 2004 by Barefoot Books Ltd
This paperback edition published in 2004

This book is printed on 100% acid-free paper
The illustrations were prepared in acrylics, pencils, and oil pastels on canvas
Design by Jennie Hoare, Bradford on Avon
Title lettering by Andrew van de Merwe, Cape Town
Typeset in Bembo 14pt
Colour separation by Grafiscan
Printed and bound in Singapore by Tien Wah Press Pte Ltd

ISBN 1901 223 264

British Cataloguing-in-Publication Data:
a catalogue record for this book is available from the British Library

3 5 7 9 8 6 4 2

Little Red Riding Hood

retold by Josephine Evetts-Secker & illustrated by Nicoletta Ceccoli

Barefoot Books
Celebrating Art and Story

In a cosy cottage on the outskirts of a sheltered village there once lived a little girl who was quiet and good. No one noticed her, until one day she appeared in a bright red cape with ribbons to fasten the hood under her chin. Now people turned their heads on the village street and everyone delighted to see her. From that day on, everyone called her Little Red Riding Hood.

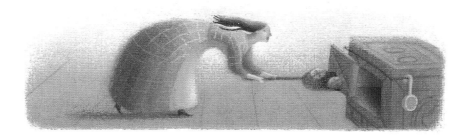

Wearing her bright cape, Little Red Riding Hood loved to visit her grandmother, and the old woman always looked forward to her coming, for she lived all alone in the middle of the forest, beyond the village. It was she who had made the cape, stitch by stitch, for her darling granddaughter's birthday.

One morning, when baking was finished, Little Red Riding Hood's mother suggested that since her grandmother was sick, Little Red Riding Hood must take her some fresh bread, some new butter and some sweet elderberry wine.

As she filled the round basket and covered it with a white linen cloth, she said, 'Now Little Red Riding Hood, be a good girl and do exactly as I say. Follow the path from our cottage to Granny's, without straying from it for one moment. Go straight there, and after a short visit, come home directly, well before dusk. Walk very carefully with the basket and watch your feet so that you don't trip over. Don't pry into Granny's things, and show her what a well-behaved little girl you are.'

Little Red Riding Hood nodded, promising to obey. She set off cautiously, making sure that the wine did not splash about in the flask.

The journey usually took no more than half an hour, so she could reach the cottage by noon. She walked steadily until she entered the cool forest. Then she slowed down and pulled her red cloak about her.

Just as she did so, a big wolf appeared on the path, blocking her way. His eyes gleamed and his long teeth sparkled as he greeted her,

'Good morning, Little Red Riding Hood.'

The young girl knew nothing about wolves, so she answered politely,

'Good morning to you too, Mr Wolf.'

'Where are you going on such a lovely spring day?' he asked.

'To visit my sick grandmother,' she replied.

'I wonder what secret things you are hiding in your round basket,' he teased.

'Oh, some freshly baked bread, some new butter and some sweet elderberry wine,' she offered. 'I helped my mother make them.'

Her red cloak shone for a moment, caught in a ray of sun through the green leaves.

'I do hope that you don't have to carry that heavy basket a long way — where does Granny live?' the cunning wolf enquired.

'Not far. It's the only cottage for miles, beside the Three Oaks, sheltered by a hazel hedge. You must know it.'

Licking his lips, the happy wolf offered to keep her company for a while, and they set off together in silence.

Suddenly the wolf stopped, pricked up his ears and exclaimed, 'Listen! How beautifully the birds are singing this morning.' Little Red Riding Hood also stopped to listen. She had never noticed birdsong in the woods before. How strange! She must tell grandmother about it.

The wily wolf smiled and they set off again, deep in thought. Watching her out of the corner of his eye, the wolf soon stopped again, when they came to a fork in the path.

'Do you ever take flowers to Granny?' he asked, and before she could reply he pointed up the left-hand path, saying, 'If you go that way, you will find a forest clearing full of flowers, red and white and — Oh, have you never seen them? Then you must run there straight away and pick a posy for Granny.'

Little Red Riding Hood gazed to the left, and gazed to the right, then back to the left path, thinking how much she would love to pick flowers. Then she said, 'If I put my basket down here at the fork in the path, I can come back to it and easily find my way again to Grandmother's house.' The wolf was delighted and encouraged her, 'Yes, of course! And I'll run and let Granny know that you are on your way.'

So Little Red Riding Hood went up the left path a little way, and seeing the promised flowers, she ran over to them and started to pick some, straying further and further from the path and deeper and deeper into the forest. She had never ever known such pleasure as she reached out after each bright flower. She looked like a flower herself in the midst of the clearing, in her bright red cape. So thought the wolf as he watched her. And then with a grin he dropped down on his four paws and ran off at high speed straight to the old lady's cottage, behind the hazel hedge.

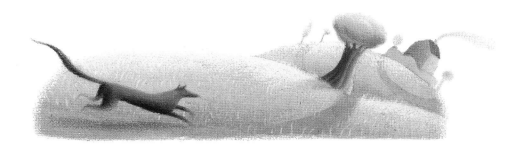

The wolf knocked at the door loudly, rousing the grandmother from her nap. 'Who is there?' she asked. The wily old wolf whispered, 'It's me, Little Red Riding Hood — with a gift for you.' So the old lady called out, 'Then come in my dear. The door isn't locked. Just lift the latch.' No sooner was the door open than the wolf jumped in, bounded across the room to the bed, and devoured the weak old woman. He laughed as he dressed up in her largest nightgown and tried to pull her nightcap over his head. Then he lay down in her bed, drew the curtains around him, and waited.

The sun climbed high in the sky as Little Red Riding Hood picked flowers, and it was casting short shadows when she found that she had gathered so many that she couldn't possibly carry them all. She took what she could and found her way back to her basket and the path to her grandmother's house. She ran so hard that the wine splashed high up the flask, and when she reached the cottage she dashed straight in, for the door had been left open, ready for her.

She rushed over to her grandmother's bed, quite out of breath, calling out, 'Granny, Granny! Look what I've brought for you.'

But her grandmother did not reply, even as Little Red Riding Hood pulled back the curtains. No delighted granny sat up or stretched out her arms to welcome her dear child. In fact, her grandmother could scarcely be seen under her bonnet with the sheets pulled right up to her chin. So Little Red Riding Hood lifted the covers.

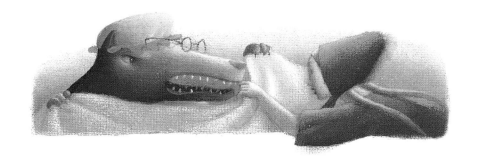

Imagine her surprise!

    'O Grandmother! What big ears you have.'

    'All the better to hear you with, my dear.'

    'O Grandmother! What big eyes you have!'

    'All the better to see you with, my dear.'

    'O Grandmother! What big hands you have!'

    'All the better to hold you with, my dear.'

    'O Grandmother! What terrible teeth you have!'

    'All the better to eat you with, my dear!'

    So cried the wolf as he pounced on Little Red Riding Hood and gobbled her up.

    Bloated and exhausted, the wolf fell back on the bed, in a loud, snoring sleep.

Just then, the huntsman was passing by the open door, stalking his prey. He heard an unfamiliar sound and came closer. Amazed by the thundering snore, he peered in to the cottage to see how the old lady was. There on the bed lay the big greedy beast that he had been pursuing for a long time. He raised his gun to make an end of him, but as he prepared to shoot, he saw the huge belly of the wolf move, and he guessed what had been swallowed.

Quickly, he took his knife from its sheath and cut open the belly with care. Immediately he recognised the red cape. Then a white little face appeared, and a very frightened girl jumped out, followed by her trembling Grandmother.

Neither old woman nor young girl were hurt, but they were relieved to be safely back in daylight. 'How dark and fearful it is inside the wolf,' Little Red Riding Hood exclaimed. Then, seeing that he had been cut wide open, she had an idea. 'I'll fill up that big dark belly with rocks.'

The huntsman helped her carry sharp rocks from the pile under the oak trees, and before the wolf could wake up, they had stuffed him and stitched him up again.

As soon as the wolf awoke, he sprang up from the bed and crashed down on to the floor, dead as a stone. The huntsman drew out his knife again, skinned the wolf, threw the pelt over his shoulder and carried it back home with him.

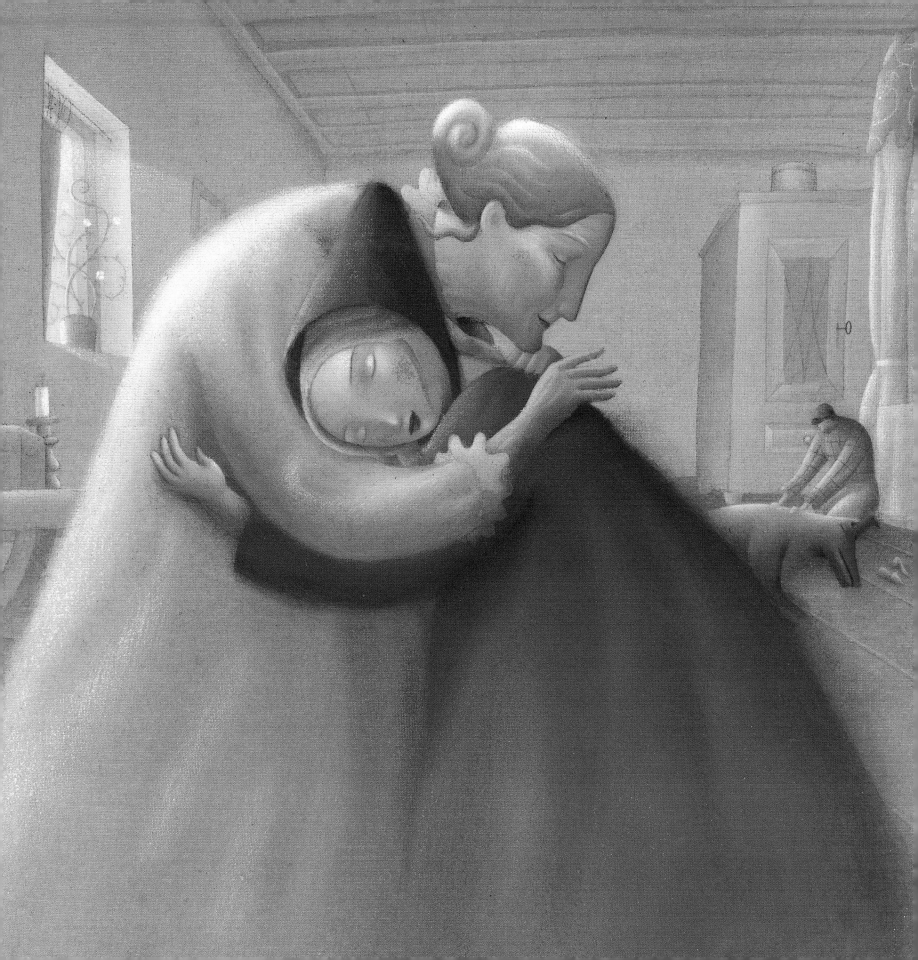

Little Red Riding Hood and her grandmother sat down together to feast on the fresh bread, the new butter and the sweet elderberry wine, while they talked of their day's adventure. Little Red Riding Hood told her granny about the birdsong and the beautiful flowers and as she shared these good things, she wondered whether she would ever meet another wolf in the forest, and if so, what would she do then?